MW00897064

For Paul
—Jen

Text Copyright © 2019 Jennifer Sattler
Illustration Copyright © 2019 Jennifer Sattler

All rights reserved. No part of this book may be reproduced in any manner without the express written consent of the publisher, except in the case of brief excerpts in critical reviews and articles. All inquiries should be addressed to:

Sleeping Bear Press™
2395 South Huron Parkway, Suite 200
Ann Arbor, MI 48104
www.sleepingbearpress.com

Printed and bound in the United States.

10 9 8 7 6 5 4 3

Library of Congress Cataloging-in-Publication Data

Names: Sattler, Jennifer Gordon, author, illustrator.
Title: One red sock / written and Illustrated by Jennifer Sattler.
Description: Ann Arbor, MI: Sleeping Bear Press, [2019] | Summary: When a little purple hippo cannot find the mate for her red sock, she tries everything in her sock drawer in order to be fashionable—or at least to match.
Identifiers: LCCN 2019004064 | ISBN 9781534110267 (hardcover)
Subjects: | CYAC: Stories in rhyme. | Socks—Fiction. | Hippopotamus—Fiction.
Classification: LCC PZ8.3.S2385 One 2019 | DDC [E]—dc23
LC record available at https://lccn.loc.gov/2019004064

One Red Sock

Jennifer Sattler

In a big pink chair
in a room full of dots . . .

sat a purple hippo
wearing one red sock.

"It looks funny this way.
This just will not do."

So she put on another sock.
This one was . . .

Blue!

"I have to be fashionable
or I cannot be seen!"

So she put on another sock.
This one was . . .

Green!

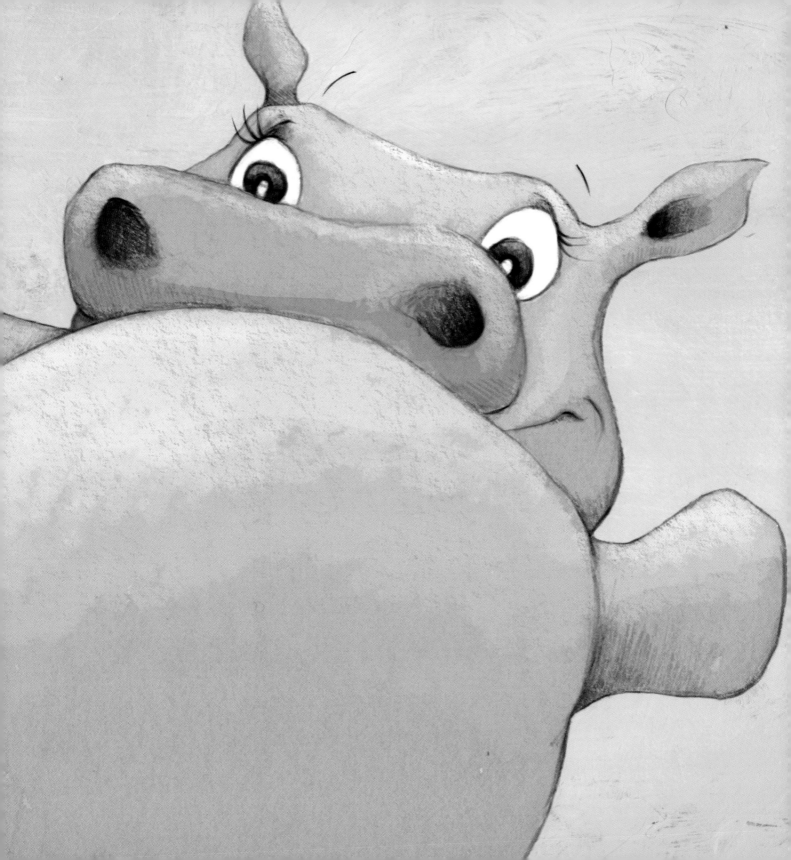

She stuck out her chin.
"This won't ruin my day!"

So she put on another sock.
This one was . . .

Gray!

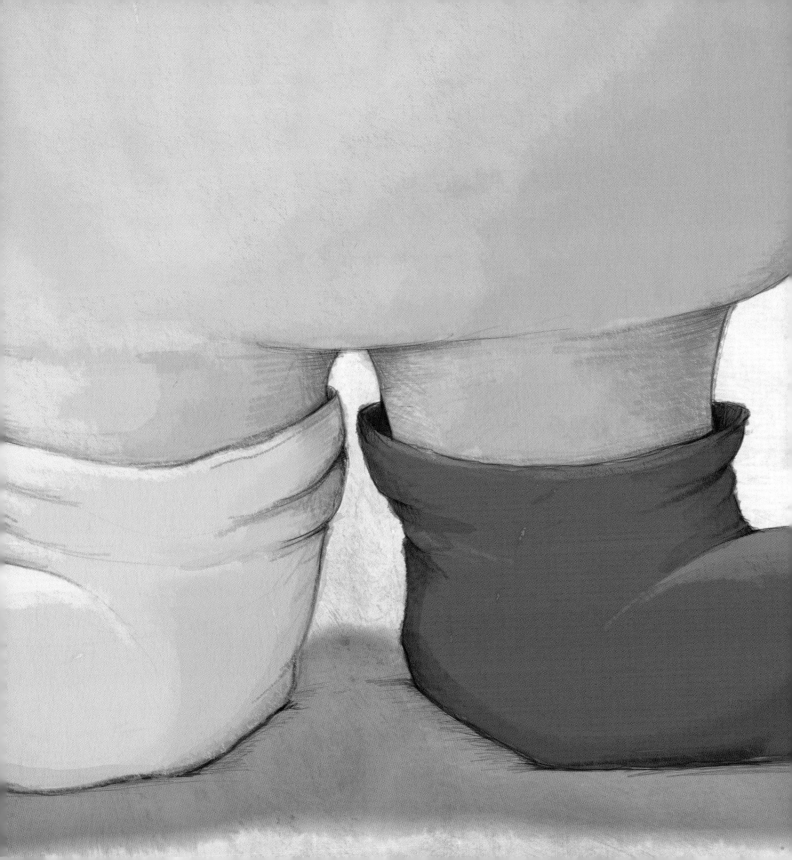

The Color Purple

Dress For Success

For The Love of Socks!

"This is driving me crazy!
It just isn't right!"

So she put on another sock.
This one was . . .

white!

She was losing her patience.
She told herself, "Think!"

So she put on another sock.
This one was . . .

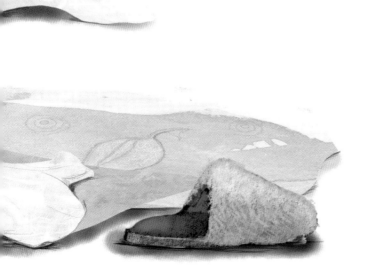

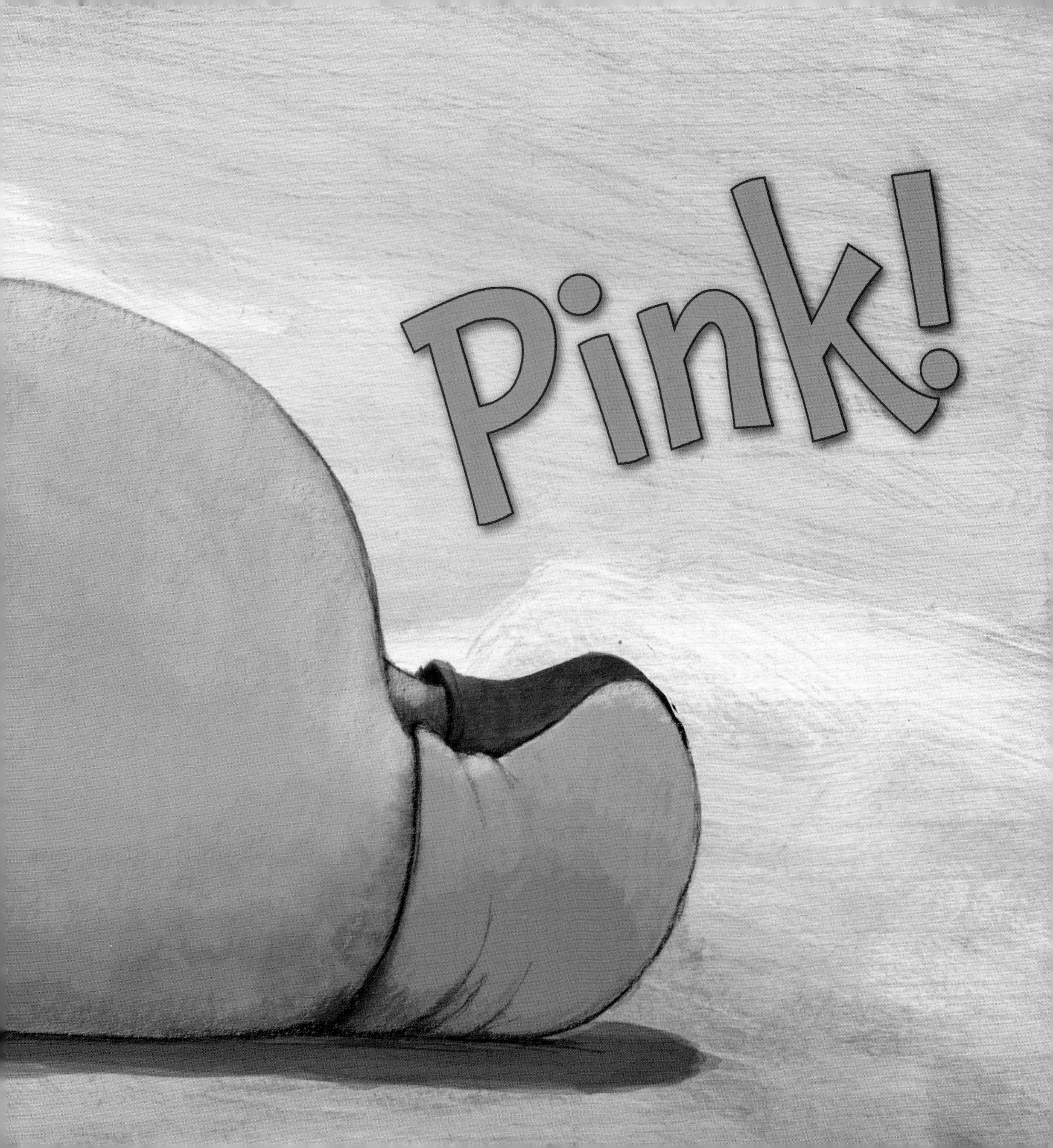
Pink!

"Well, I hope this one works.
It's the last one I've got."

And she pulled on a sock with . . .

"Well, it's not perfect.
And it's definitely not red."

"But at least it matches my room!" she said.

So she tottered off happy, though her socks weren't a pair. And the other red sock?

It had always been there.

A Note From Jennifer Sattler

The little purple hippo wants her socks to match so that everything will look just right. She is trying to be perfect. And trying to be perfect is frustrating.

Have you ever tried to draw a flower but it ends up looking like a bunch of balloons?

Sometimes I don't get things right the first time. Or the fourth time . . . or the 123rd time. But once in a while, on the second or the fifth or the 124th time, something so silly, so wonderful, and so surprising will happen that it becomes the *new* perfect. It's better than the thing I was trying to do!

So maybe the next time you're getting dressed or drawing a picture or telling a story or baking a cake or building a spaceship and it doesn't go right the first time . . . keep trying. Because you know what? You just might find something amazing that you weren't even looking for. Like our little hippo's perfect polka dot sock.